A *PAIR* of *PEARS* and an *ORANGE*

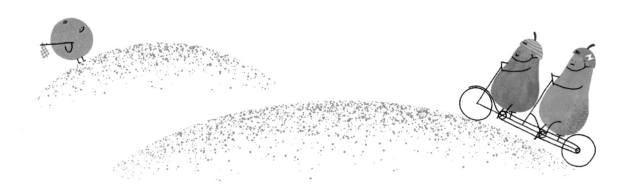

For Nicole

The illustrations in this book were rendered digitally.
Typeset in Sagona. Hand-lettering by Anna McGregor.

Scribble, an imprint of Scribe Publications
18–20 Edward Street, Brunswick, Victoria 3056, Australia
2 John Street, Clerkenwell, London, WC1N 2ES, UK
3754 Pleasant Ave, Suite 100, Minneapolis, Minnesota 55409, USA

Text & illustrations copyright © Anna McGregor, 2021
Design by Anna McGregor

First published by Scribble, 2021

MIX
Paper from
responsible sources
FSC® C016973

This book is printed with vegetable-soy based inks, on FSC® certified paper and other controlled material from responsibly managed forests, ensuring that the supply chain from forest to end-user is chain of custody certified. Printed and bound in China by 1010.

9781922310750 (Australian hardback)
9781913348748 (UK hardback)
9781950354702 (US hardback)

Catalogue records for this title are available from the National Library of Australia and the British Library

scribblekidsbooks.com
scribblekidsbooks

We acknowledge the Wurundjeri People of the Kulin Nation are the first and continuing custodians of the land on which our books are created. Sovereignty has never been ceded. We pay our respects to Elders past, present, and emerging, and to all First Nations people.

A PAIR of PEARS and an ORANGE

Written and illustrated by

Anna McGregor

SCRIBBLE

A pair of pears rocked on a seesaw.

A pair of pears played ping-pong.

And a pair of pears rode their tandem bike.

Until one day ...

... someone new wanted to join their fun.

'Room for one more?'
asked Orange.

'Sure!' said Little Pear.

But Big Pear was not so sure.

So, a pair of pears and an orange played noughts-and-crosses.

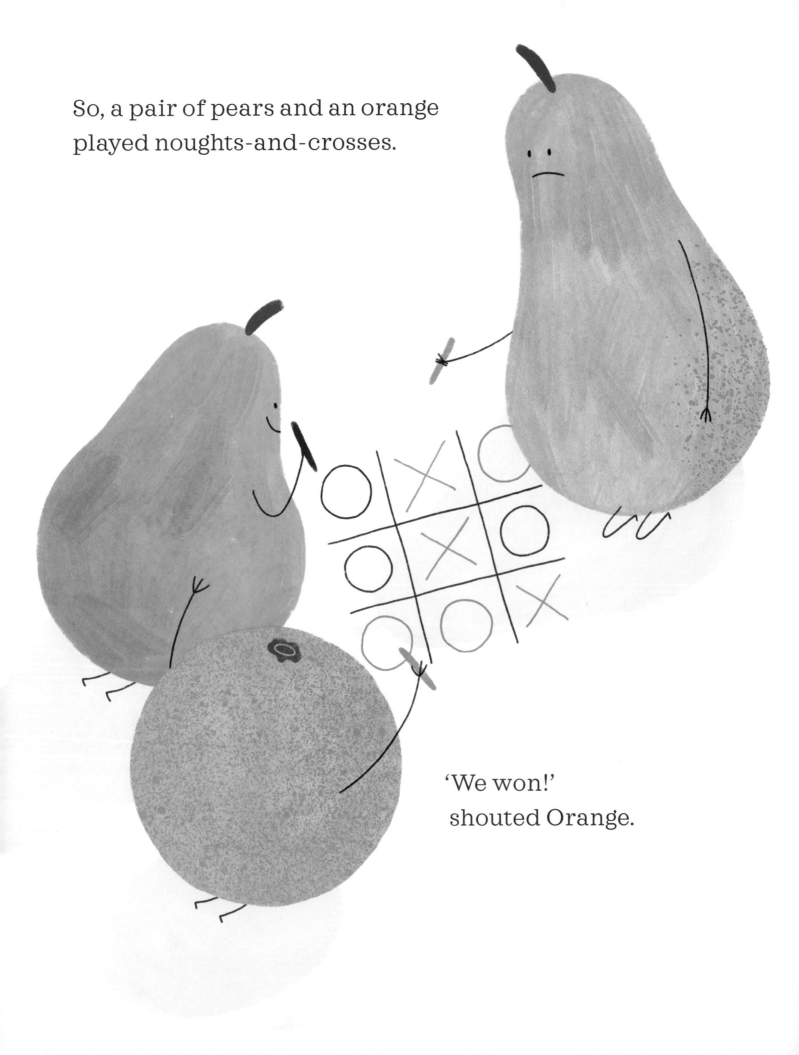

'We won!'
shouted Orange.

A pair of pears and an orange rowed a boat.

'We're going
in circles!'
said Big Pear.

And a pair of pears and an orange played tug of war.

None of the pears' games worked for three,
but Orange and Little Pear didn't seem to notice.

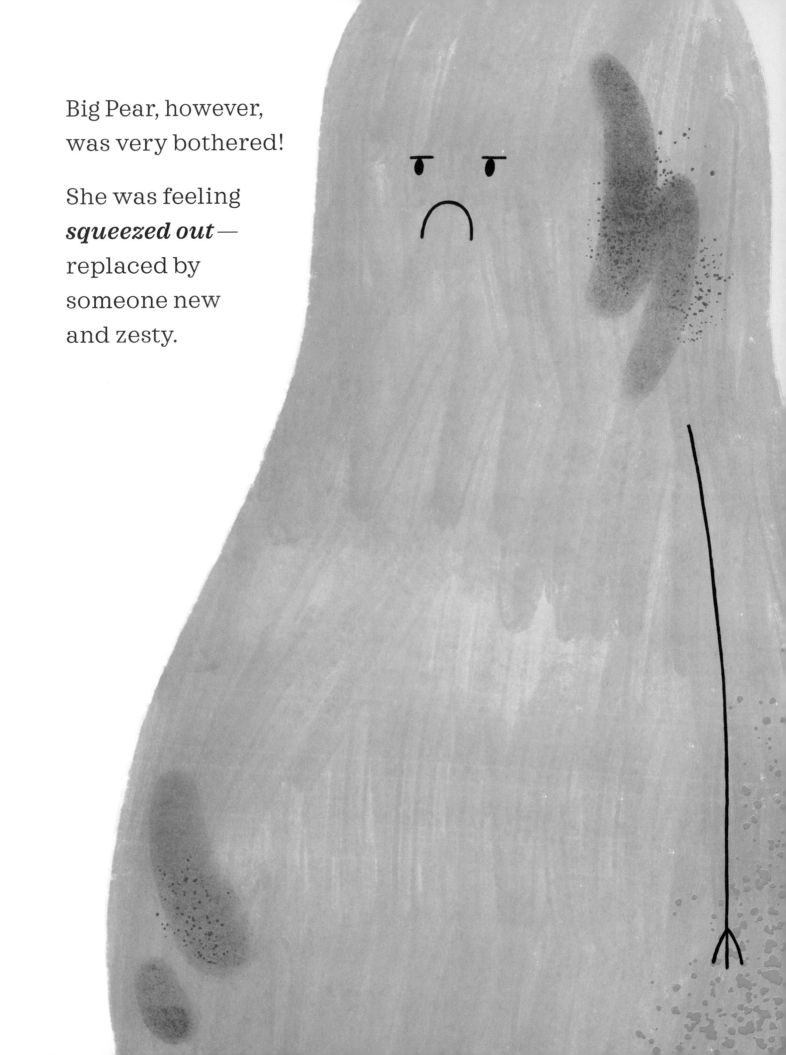

Big Pear, however,
was very bothered!

She was feeling
squeezed out—
replaced by
someone new
and zesty.

'*Orange* you glad I'm here?' joked Orange.

'You're so funny,' said Little Pear.

Big Pear had had enough.
She left to find someone else to play with.

'Look, she's
disap*pear*ing on us!'
joked Orange.

But this time
Little Pear wasn't
laughing.

Three peas played jump rope.

'Hi there,' said Big Pear.
'Can I join?'

So, three peas and a pear played piggy in the middle.

Three peas and a pear made a cheerleading pyramid.

And that evening, three peas and a pear
tucked themselves into their pod.

But Big Pear didn't fit in ...

As the peas slept, cosy together in their pod,
Big Pear lay awake thinking about her old friends.

She missed
Little Pear's
kindness.

She even missed
Orange's bad jokes.

The very next day, Big Pear
went back to her old friends
and asked if she could play
with them again.

'It hasn't been the
same without you,'
said Orange.

'We missed you!'
said Little Pear.

Then Big Pear taught them all
the new games she'd learnt ...

... perfect for three.

'That looks fun!
Can I join in?'